Another Sommer-Time Story™

PROUD
ROOSTER
and Little Hen

By Carl Sommer
Illustrated by Greg Budwine

Advance • HOUSTON
PUBLSHING, INC.

Permissions
Advance Publishing, Inc.
6950 Fulton St.
Houston, TX 77022

www.advancepublishing.com

First Edition
Printed in Malaysia

Library of Congress Cataloging-in-Publication Data

Sommer, Carl, 1930-
  Proud Rooster and Little Hen / by Carl Sommer; illustrated by Greg Budwine. -- 1st ed.
   p. cm. -- (Another Sommer-Time Story)
  Summary: Proud Rooster never listens to anyone's advice, until finally he gets into serious trouble.
   Cover title: Carl Sommer's Proud Rooster and Little Hen.
   ISBN 1-57537-010-7 (hardcover: alk. paper). -- ISBN 1-57537-060-3 (library binding: alk. paper)
   [1. Behavior Fiction. 2. Roosters Fiction. 3. Domestic animals Fiction.] I. Budwine, Greg, ill. II. Title. III. Carl Sommer's Proud Rooster and Little Hen. IV. Series: Sommer, Carl, 1930- Another Sommer-Time Story.
PZ7.S69235r 2000   99-35280
[E]--dc21   CIP

PROUD
ROOSTER
and Little Hen

The sun shone, flowers bloomed, and the meadows turned bright green. The long, cold winter was finally over.

"Yippeeee!" yelled Little Rooster. "We can finally go outside and play ball again."

"I'm glad too," said Little Hen.

As Papa and Mama watched everyone play, Mama said, "I hope Little Rooster will start learning to obey."

"So do I," sighed Papa. "Lately, Little Rooster has been getting into all kinds of trouble for not listening."

In fact, around the farm Little Rooster had another name—Proud Rooster. The only one he ever listened to was himself.

Papa and Mama often tried to teach him, but Proud Rooster would just stick out his chest. He was not going to listen to *anyone!*

"Sometimes little roosters have to learn things the hard way," Papa would say. "And sometimes they learn them when it is too late."

Until now, Proud Rooster had managed to stay out of really big trouble. He did not know it, but things were about to change.

It all started one bright sunny day when Proud Rooster and Little Hen walked by a strawberry patch.

"Wow!" yelled Proud Rooster. "Look at all those delicious strawberries."

"You'd better not eat them," warned Little Hen. "They aren't ripe. Mama told us, 'Green strawberries will make us sick.'"

But do you think Proud Rooster listened? No! Not Proud Rooster!

"I'll just take one little bite," said Proud Rooster.

But the green strawberries tasted so good, that one little bite became two little bites. And so it went, until Proud Rooster had stuffed his tummy full of green strawberries.

That night Proud Rooster could not eat his supper. He was sick—terribly sick.

"Ohhhhhh!" groaned Proud Rooster over and over again. "My stomach hurts!"

After a few days, Proud Rooster felt better. He left the house and went to play with his friends. As he came strutting by, they were talking about climbing trees.

"I can climb higher than anyone," he bragged.

Tom Turkey pointed to the largest tree on the farm. "I dare you to climb to the top of that tree!"

"That's easy," boasted Proud Rooster.
"Don't do it," warned Little Hen.
"You could fall and get hurt," said Lucy Lamb.
But do you think Proud Rooster listened? No!
Not Proud Rooster!

Proud Rooster stuck out his chest and walked up to the tree.

"Just watch *me!*" he crowed as he began to climb. "I'll show you that *I'm* the best climber on the whole farm."

Up, up, went Proud Rooster.
"Be careful!" called Little Hen.
"Be quiet!" yelled Proud Rooster.   "You know
I'm the best climber around."
Higher and higher he went.

Proud Rooster looked down and saw everyone talking. "They must be talking about how good a climber I am," he said.

They were not. They were saying how foolish he was for trying to show off.

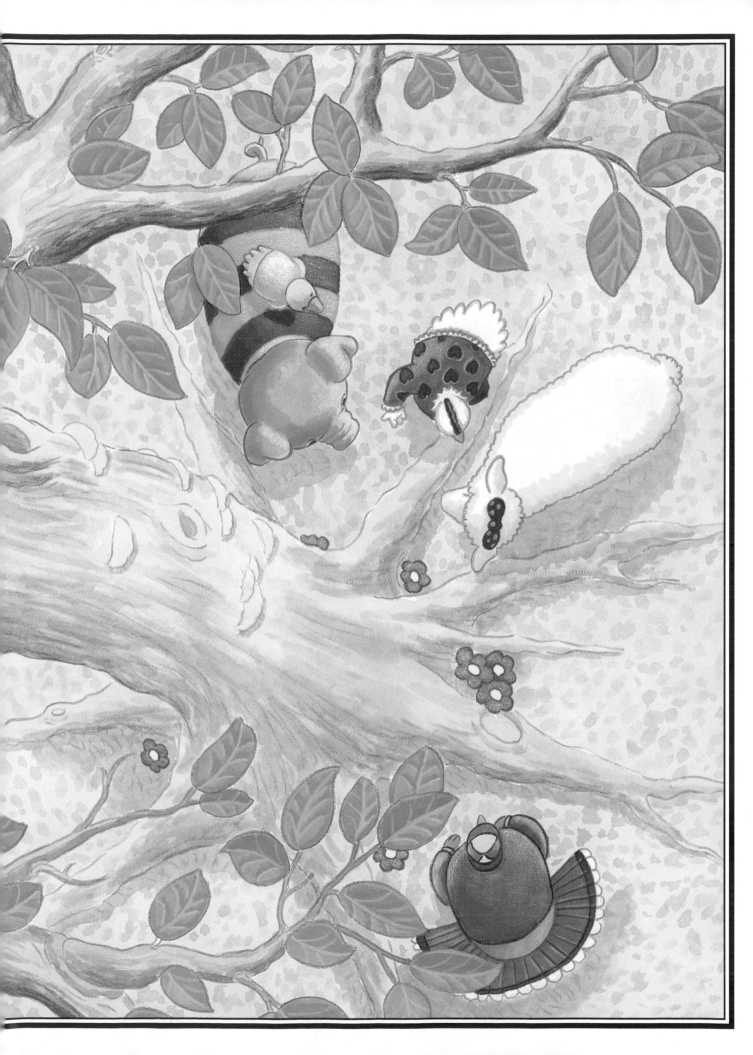

"Only three more branches to go," said Proud Rooster to himself. "Then everyone will know that *I* am the best climber!"

Just as Proud Rooster put his foot on the next branch, there was a loud CRACK!!!

The branch snapped. Proud Rooster lost his balance and began to fall.

"Help!!!! Help!!!!" he screamed. "I'm falling!"

But no one could help him.

Down, down went Proud Rooster.
CLACK! CLUNK! CRASH!
He fell fast, hitting tree limbs all along the way. Finally, there was a loud THUD!!! Proud Rooster had hit the ground.

"Ouch!" cried Lucy Lamb.

"Are you okay?" asked Pinky Pig.

But not a sound came from Proud Rooster.

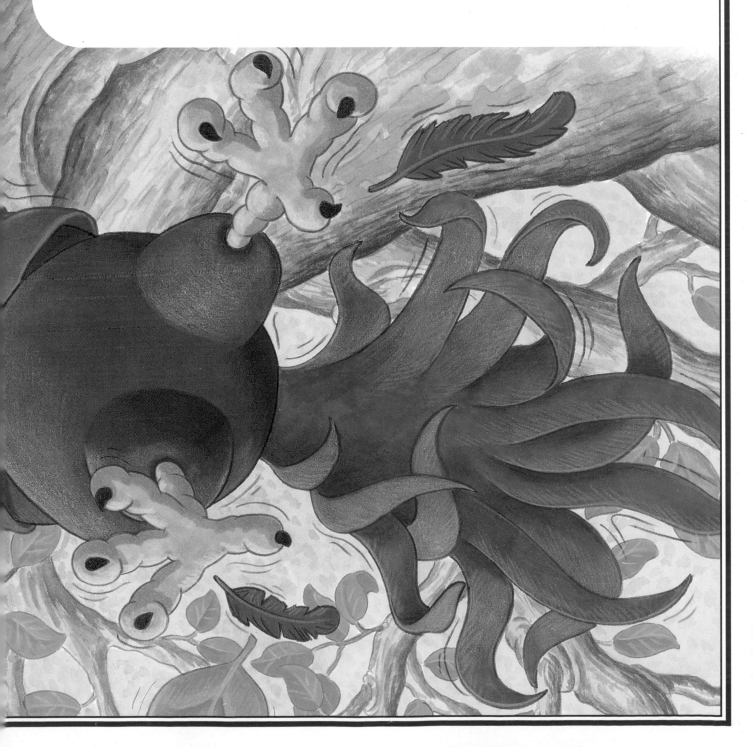

Little Hen cried out, "Hurry! Someone get Dr. Owl!"

Tom Turkey ran as fast as he could to get help. Dr. Owl came quickly. He looked at Proud Rooster's eyes and checked his heart. Then Dr. Owl let out a sigh. "He'll be okay, but he'll be sore for a long time. He broke his arms and legs, and his head is badly hurt."

They rushed Proud Rooster to the hospital. After the doctors had examined him, they bandaged him from head to toe.

"Ohhhhh!!!" cried Proud Rooster. "My head hurts! And my arms and legs hurt, too! Everything hurts!"

Time passed, and Proud Rooster finally went home. But he had to stay in bed for a long time. "Ohhhhhh! How I wish I could be outside playing with my friends," moaned Proud Rooster. "Now I have to lie in this bed until I get better."

It was wintertime before Proud Rooster was well enough to go outside. He was so happy when he stepped out on the porch that he yelled, "Hoorayyyyy!!! Now I can go outside and play again."

He joined his friends at the pond who were having fun throwing snowballs. Then Proud Rooster got an idea. "Let's go slide on the ice."

"Oh no!" said Pinky Pig. "See that sign?"

Tom Turkey read it. "Thin Ice. Stay Away!"

With all the bad things that had happened to Proud Rooster, do you think he listened? No! Not Proud Rooster!

"We'll go only where the ice is thick," said Proud Rooster.

"But it's dangerous," warned Little Hen.

Proud Rooster got mad at Little Hen. "Keep quiet! You always want to spoil my fun."

Away went Proud Rooster. At first he was very careful. But the more he slid, the more fun he had. And the more fun he had, the farther out he slid.

"Wheeee!" shouted Proud Rooster. "This is fun! Why don't you come and join me? It's safe out here. You don't have to be afraid."

But no one listened. They knew better.

"The ice is thin out there," warned Pinky Pig.

"Look out!" Tom Turkey shouted. "The ice is beginning to crack!"

The others saw it, too. Lucy Lamb yelled, "You're going to fall in!"

But do you think Proud Rooster listened? No! Not Proud Rooster!

"You're all a bunch of babies!" yelled Proud Rooster. "Watch *me!*"

He ran as fast as he could and slid far across the ice, yelling, "Wheeeeeeee! This is fun!"

Then it happened. CRACK!!! went the ice.

Down went Proud Rooster into the freezing water.

"Help! Help!" he cried. "Get me out of here! The water is ice c-c-c-c-cold!"

Proud Rooster struggled and struggled to get out, but the ice kept breaking. "Hurry up and get me out of here!" screamed Proud Rooster. "I'm freeeeezing!"

Everyone wanted to help, but they could not reach him.

"If only we had a rope!" yelled Dollie Duck.

"That's it!" exclaimed Little Hen. "I'll get a rope!" Off she ran as fast as she could.

In a flash, Little Hen was back. She threw the rope to Proud Rooster and yelled, "Grab the rope, and we'll pull you out!"

Proud Rooster was so cold that he could hardly move. He struggled to reach the rope. Finally he was able to grab it.

Little Hen, Pinky Pig, Tom Turkey, and Lucy Lamb yelled, "Hold on!" as they pulled on the rope. Dollie Duck cheered them on.

They tugged and yanked until they finally pulled Proud Rooster out of the freezing water.

Proud Rooster was so cold that he was too weak to move. They lifted him onto Pinky Pig, and Little Hen covered him with her coat. Then they struggled through the deep snow to take him home.

When Papa and Mama saw Proud Rooster, they quickly called Dr. Owl.

"Rush him to the hospital," said Dr. Owl. "I'll meet you there."

Papa and Mama bundled up Proud Rooster
and rushed him to the hospital.

After Dr. Owl examined Proud Rooster, he stood outside the room and gave everyone the bad news. "I don't know if Proud Rooster is going to make it. He's suffering from a bad case of frostbite."

Although Proud Rooster was unable to move, he could hear just fine. When he heard what Dr. Owl said, he became so afraid that his insides began to shake.

Proud Rooster thought about all the trouble he had gotten into. "It's all because I was proud and didn't listen. I've learned my lesson. From now on I'm listening!"

Then Proud Rooster remembered what Papa had said over and over. "Sometimes little roosters have to learn things the hard way. And sometimes they learn them when it is too late."

"Too late?" cried Proud Rooster softly. "Have I learned my lesson too late?"

Proud Rooster tried to move, but he was too weak. Finally, using all his strength, he whispered, "Papa!"

Just outside the room, Papa thought he had

heard a sound. "What was that?" he asked.
"I'm quite sure it sounded like Little Rooster!"
said Mama.
Everyone rushed into the room.

There was Proud Rooster, barely able to open his eyes, but he was ready to talk! "I'm sorry for being so proud and not listening," he whispered. "Papa, is it too late?"

Papa wrapped his arms around his son and said, "No, Little Rooster. You have learned to listen just in time."